Sam
and the
Apricot Tree

by Anne Pilmoor
Illustrated by Lorenzo Sabbatini

Sam rubbed the stinging scratches on his arms and legs. He looked at the huge broken branch lying on the ground and feared the trouble that lay ahead. . . .

The apricot tree in the orchard at the bottom of the garden was Sam's favourite. It was the biggest and oldest tree of the lot. Its fruit were the first to ripen in the early summer and every year there were . . .

*enough apricots for them to give
baskets and baskets away to friends
and neighbours;*

enough to make cool, delicious apricot sorbet all through the summer;

enough to make loads of their
favourite apricot tarts;

enough for Grandma to make bottles
and bottles of dark, golden jam;

enough for Sam's lunchbox;

enough for the birds to have a little feast!

Even better, the apricot tree's branches were the best for climbing. Sam's special branch was low down and shaped just like a horse's back. He loved to straddle it and pretend he was riding his horse across the prairie. The branch would rock gently as he trotted and would shake violently when he galloped.

Now Sam wished he had not made the horse gallop so fast. He could still hear the ear-splitting crack as the branch tore away from the tree.

Sam knew that bandages had helped to keep Jo's arm straight until it was 'fixed'.

'What a brilliant idea! I'll bandage the branch to the tree, and maybe it will grow back again . . .' he thought, 'just like Jo's arm.'

Sam rummaged through the first aid box for the longest bandage he could find.

There were yards and yards of it!
First he struggled to lift the branch
off the ground. It was SO heavy.
Then, every time he managed to lift
it up and he tried to get the
bandage around it, it would
flop over and fall to the ground.

'Oh dear!' cried Sam.
'What can I do?'

'Maybe the bandages weren't strong enough,' he thought. 'Rope might work better. . . . **What a brilliant idea!** I'll fasten the branch back with rope, just like the ropes that keep the logs together on the raft by the lake. . . .'

Sam found a good, strong rope in the garden shed. First he struggled to lift the branch off the ground. It was SO heavy. Then, every time he managed to lift it up and he tried to wind the rope around it, it would flop over and fall to the ground.

'Oh dear!' cried Sam. 'What can I do?'

'I know . . .' thought Sam as he stared at the wire running through the chain fence down the side of the yard. 'I'll fasten the branch back with wire. Wire is tough and strong. **What a brilliant idea!**' he chuckled.

Sam found a reel of wire in the garage. First he struggled to lift the branch off the ground. It was SO heavy. Then, every time he managed to lift it up and he tried to get the wire around it, the branch would flop over and fall to the ground.

'Oh dear!' cried Sam. 'What can I do?'

Sam stared hopelessly at the sharp splinters on the broken branch. He remembered how Dad had used wood glue to fix his sock drawer. It was still as sturdy as a rock. He was sure the glue would work. **'What a brilliant idea!'** he said to himself as he went off to find the glue.

Sam found a big tub of it in the workshop. First he painted the glue on the torn parts of the tree and the branch. Then he struggled to lift up the branch. It was **SO** heavy. It seemed to work better when he sat on the ground and pushed the branch in place with his feet.

'Hurrah!' he thought. 'This is going to work!' and he held the branch in place with his feet until his legs started to ache. Slowly he inched his feet away. It seemed the branch was fixed, when, suddenly, the branch teetered and fell to the ground with a crash!

'Oh dear!' cried Sam. 'What can I do?'

*'**I have a brilliant idea!**' said Sam.*
'Why didn't I think about it in the first place?'

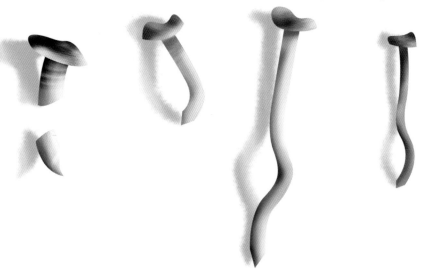

*Sam found a tin of nails and a big strong hammer in the workshop. 'I'm going to nail the branch back to the tree, just like the panels of the garden shed are nailed to the frame.' He grinned. First Sam struggled to lift the branch off the ground. It was **SO** heavy. When he eventually lifted it off the ground he picked up a good looking nail and started to hammer. He hammered and hammered, but the nail just would not go through. He tried a thinner nail, then a longer nail, a shorter nail and a fatter one, but none of them worked. . . . . His shoulder hurt from propping the branch up as he hammered. Just when he stopped to give his shoulder a rest, the branch suddenly swayed and crashed to the ground.*

'Oh dear!' cried Sam. 'What can I do?'

Sam took a sweeping look across the
back garden. He noticed a few bricks left
over from the time they had paved the patio. . . .

'**I have a brilliant
idea!**' he said. 'I'll
use the bricks to prop up
the branch. Maybe the sap
from the branch will help it to
stick together. . . .'

Sam carried the bricks over to the tree. They did a
brilliant job of propping the branch up. It looked like
a proper tree again. Sam was sure this idea was
going to work, until the first gust of wind unsettled
the branch and it flopped over and fell to the ground.

'Oh dear!' cried Sam. 'What can I do?'

'I've got **an idea!**' he thought. 'Not a brilliant one, but I hope it will work.'

Sam went to the study where Mum was working on the computer. The papers were shooting out of the printer and she looked pleased.

'Hi Sam,' called Mum.

Sam shuffled his feet. He twisted his arms inside out.
He took an enormous breath and said,

'Mum, please come with me to the orchard. . . .
I have something to show you.'

Mum went quiet and pale as she stared at the mess. . . . She saw half a tree on the ground, bandages, rope, wire, nails, bricks, tools and leaves scattered everywhere.

'I have a confession to make,' said Sam. 'I'm really sorry, Mum. I have ruined the best tree in the orchard.'

Mum looked upset. She put her hand on Sam's shoulder. 'I know you are sorry, Sam, and I am, too. You know I will always forgive you, but what do you think we could do so that we can have . . .

enough apricots for us to give baskets and baskets to our friends and neighbours?

Enough to make cool apricot sorbet all through the summer?

Enough to make all our favourite apricot tarts?

Enough for Grandma to make bottles and bottles of dark, golden jam?

Enough for your lunchbox?

Enough for the birds to have a little feast?'

Sam thought for a while.

'**I've got a brilliant idea!**' he whispered. 'I can plant another apricot tree in the orchard. . . .'

Sam held his piggy bank tight as he inspected every apricot tree at the garden centre. They all looked so small and spindly. . . . Sam knew it was going to take a long time before any of those trees would grow enough apricots.

The nurseryman took Sam round the corner. Sam had never seen such huge trees growing in such huge pots. Then he saw what he was looking for. He recognised the blossoms on the tree. 'I'll buy that one,' he said.

He emptied his piggy bank on the counter. There were coins and notes everywhere. Sam knew exactly how much he had in the piggy bank, but the assistant seemed to take hours counting it all. The man said he would use his big truck to deliver the tree later.

Mum and Sam dug a huge hole in the ground.
They filled it with compost. Mum said it would give
the tree a good start. Sam helped to fill the hole
with soil when the tree had been planted.

'It's hard work planting a tree,' puffed Sam.

Sam looked at Mum, all hot
and sweaty. 'This tree is
going to be all right, Mum,'
he said.

'I hope it will,' she smiled.

'I know it will, because I prayed quietly as we filled the hole with soil. . . . I asked God to bless the tree, to make it grow strong so there would be . . .
enough apricots to give baskets and baskets to our friends and neighbours;
enough to make cool apricot sorbet all through the summer;
enough to make all our favourite apricot tarts;
enough for Grandma to make bottles and bottles of dark, golden jam;
enough for my lunchbox;
enough for the birds to have a little feast!'

Mum drew him closer. 'Fancy that! I said a little prayer, too. Can you guess what I prayed?' she teased. Sam shook his head.
'I thanked God for helping you to be brave enough to own up and say you were sorry for your mistake, and for helping you to think of a way to make things right. . . . **What a brilliant idea** to plant another apricot tree!' she beamed.

Suddenly Mum had a worried look on her face, as she took a big sniff.
'Oh dear!' shouted Mum, and she started to run towards the house. 'I forgot the apricot tart was still in the oven . . . !'

Saying thank you to God

by KAREN HOLFORD

This beautifully written and illustrated story
on stewardship will delight young children.
It also includes practical activities and
suggestions that will encourage children
to want to say *thank you to God*.

Also published by Autumn House

Your Angel

by Becky De Oliveira

Illustrated by Alice De Marco

Children will enjoy the stories and beautiful illustrations
about the boy who throws out a series of challenges
to his angel to show him what he looks like.
His mother handles the boy's frustration
in an unusual but remarkable way. . . .
This is sure to become a child's favourite book.

Also published by Autumn House

What Shall I Dream About?

by Becky De Oliveira
Illustrated by Chiara Varcesi

A young boy is ready for bed and asks his mother,
'What shall I dream about?' Each suggestion from
the mother is beautifully illustrated, and the best is
saved for last. This wonderful book will help each little
sleepy head drift off to a peaceful night's sleep.

Also published by Autumn House

First published in 2009 • Copyright © 2009 Autumn House Publishing (Europe) Ltd. • Author: Anne Pilmoor • Illustrator: Lorenzo Sabbatini

Published by Autumn House, Alma Park, Grantham, Lincs. Printed in Thailand